God Is On Your Side

Compiled by Marjorie Miller • Edited by Theresa Hayes

Cover Illustration by Joe Boddy

STANDARD PUBLISHING
Cincinnati, Ohio
3616

Library of Congress Cataloging-in-Publication Data

God is on your side.

   Summary: Fifteen stories, set in either Biblical
or modern times, demonstrate that God is active and
caring in our lives.
   1. Providence and government of God—Juvenile
literature. [1. God] I. Miller, Marjorie. II. Hayes,
Theresa.
BT135.G63   1986   248.8'2   86-5732
ISBN 0-87403-096-X

TABLE OF CONTENTS

GOD
CARES
ABOUT ME

Hooray for Timothy Toodles!

by Dorotha Ruthstrom

When my kite gets a tear, I fix it with tape. When my beach ball gets a hole, my father puts a patch on it. When I get cut or scraped, I wear a patch too. But I'm not like my kite, and I'm not like my beach ball.

I'm Timothy Toodles and I am wonderfully made! So, after a few days, I take off my patch, and HOORAY! I'm all grown together again.

When my stuffed dog gets mustard on his face, it stays there forever—dried up mustard. When my shoes get scuffs on the toes, they stay scuffed. But I'm not like my stuffed dog and I'm not like my scuffed shoes.

I'm Timothy Toodles and I am wonderfully made! So, when I get a black eye, my skin changes colors until HOORAY! It gets back to me.

My red wagon is always red. My green beach ball is always green. But I'm not like my wagon and I'm not like my beach ball.

I'm Timothy Toodles and I am wonderfully made! So, in summertime, I change colors. It's neat when I take off my shirt—and HOORAY! It looks like I still have one on.

When I cut my yo-yo string too short, I have to buy a new string. When I cut my doll's hair, the doll looks funny forever. When I cut my hair, I look funny too. But my hair is not like my doll's hair.

I'm Timothy Toodles and I am wonderfully made! HOORAY! I have hair that grows.

My car will always fit in its garage. My spade will always fit in its bucket. But I'm not like my car or like my spade. I'm Timothy Toodles and I am wonderfully made! Sometimes I don't fit a thing. HOORAY! New clothes for a growing me!

My kite will never fly alone. And my shoes will never walk alone. My beach ball will never bounce by itself. And my spade will never fill its bucket without my help.

But, HOORAY for me—
　　　Timothy Toodles!

I am wonderfully made and I'm getting smarter every day. I think I might be president or a race-car driver someday.

Or perhaps I'll ask God what I should be since He's the one who made WONDERFUL ME!

Let's Talk About This

1. In this story, Timothy Toodles is thanking God because he is "wonderfully made." "Wonderfully" is a hard word to say, but it is right out of the Bible. Look at Psalm 139:14. What do you think "wonderfully" means? If you take the word apart, you get "full of wonder." What does that mean?

2. In Psalm 139:14 the shepherd boy David is "praising" God. "Praising" means to thank God, to be glad for what He has done, to tell God how good He is for doing something. When you say, "Thank you, Mother, for making this yummy cake. It tastes so good and I am so happy that you made it," you are praising your mother. We can praise God like that too, and that is what Timothy Toodles is doing. What does he thank God for? How does he tell God that His creations are "full of wonder"?

3. Have you ever had a cut and watched it get better day by day? Don't you think that God created skin to be pretty wonderful? It grows back together again, sunburned skin falls off when new skin has grown to replace it, skin grows to cover our bodies, no matter how big we get, skin gives hair a place to grow, skin has little tiny holes in it so that we can sweat when we get hot (and the sweat helps us to cool down), and skin is soft and very nice to touch. Isn't skin a wonderful creation? Why don't you tell God how wonderful you think it is, and how wonderful it was of Him to create it, and thank Him for skin? Then see if you can think of some other wonderful things about yourself to thank Him for.

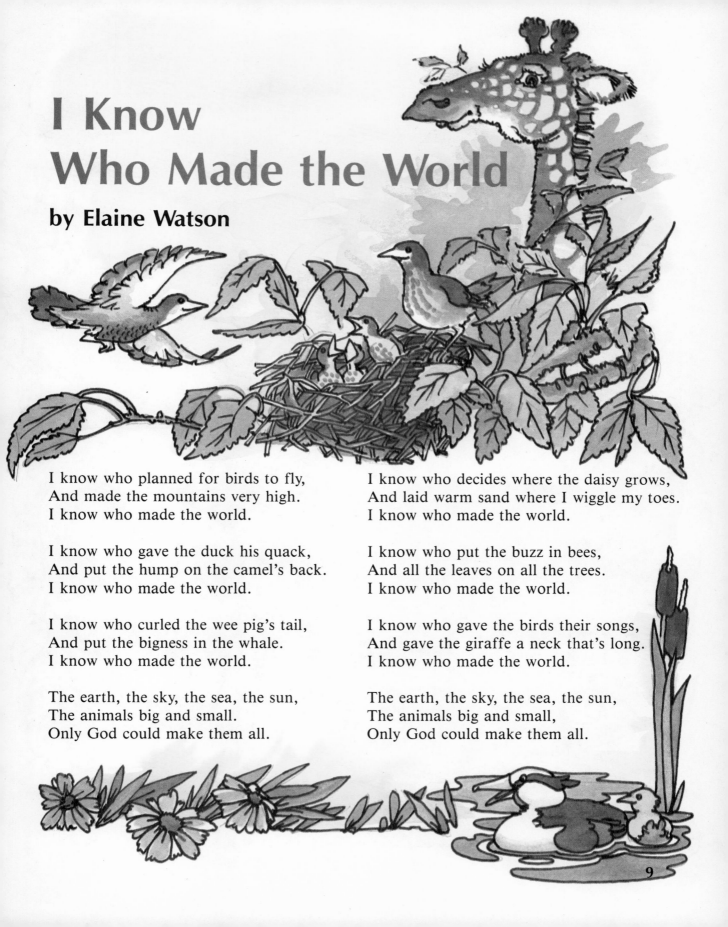

I Know Who Made the World

by Elaine Watson

I know who planned for birds to fly,
And made the mountains very high.
I know who made the world.

I know who gave the duck his quack,
And put the hump on the camel's back.
I know who made the world.

I know who curled the wee pig's tail,
And put the bigness in the whale.
I know who made the world.

The earth, the sky, the sea, the sun,
The animals big and small.
Only God could make them all.

I know who decides where the daisy grows,
And laid warm sand where I wiggle my toes.
I know who made the world.

I know who put the buzz in bees,
And all the leaves on all the trees.
I know who made the world.

I know who gave the birds their songs,
And gave the giraffe a neck that's long.
I know who made the world.

The earth, the sky, the sea, the sun,
The animals big and small,
Only God could make them all.

I know who gave the bear his growl,
And planned for the cat to say "meow."
I know who made the world.

I know who gave the zebra stripes,
And put the days between the nights.
I know who made the world.

I know who gave the turtle his shell,
And all the flowers their lovely smell.
I know who made the world.

10

I know who made the ocean so blue,
And I know who made me too.
I know who made the world.

The earth, the sky, the sea, the sun,
The animals big and small.
Only God could make them all.

And *that's* who made the world.
And now you know it too!

Let's Talk About This

1. Sometimes we can know something all our lives and never really think about it. You have probably always known that God created the world, but have you ever stopped to think what that means?

2. When we make something, we start with something. If you make a picture, you start with paper, crayons, markers, or pencils. When your mother makes a cake, she starts with flour, butter, and eggs. But when God made the world, He started with nothing. He created life, colors, sound, air, water, earth, food—and everything—out of His own mind.

3. Can you think of more things that people make, using materials that God provides? For example, we make houses and furniture out of trees that God makes. Who makes cars and trucks? Who created iron, and the fire we use to shape it? We study and read to put knowledge into our minds, but who created our minds?

4. There is a very big word we use to describe God. The word is "om-nip-o-tent." It means "unlimited power, all-mighty." It means God can do anything. How does this fact make you feel about God?

5. God *is* our friend, and He loves us very much, but we need to think of Him as more than just a friend. God is *God*. In the Bible, God introduces himself as "I AM" (Exodus 3:14). This means that God *has* always existed, and *will* always exist. There is no beginning or end to God. We need to have a proper respect for God. How can you show your respect for God?

Chirpy

by Sally Grant Conan

Answer me when I pray, O God, my defender! When I was in trouble, you helped me. Be kind to me now and hear my prayer.

—Psalm 4:1

Dear God, this is Tommy, and I have a problem. My teacher, Mr. Marlow, wants us to write a report on our favorite pet. You know I am the only one in the entire class who does not have a pet! Mother says it's hard enough getting money to feed my brothers and sisters and me. She says there is nothing left to spend on a pet. And besides, Mother says, "They are too much bother and they carry germs." What really made me feel sad was when I asked my friend Timmy if I could write about one of his goldfish (he has two) and he said, "No way!"

God, I know this is quite a problem, but you have worked out bigger problems. You even made the world! So, dear God, if it isn't too much trouble, could you please help me find a pet?

We have until this Friday. Thanks for listening.

Dear God, I heard him when I woke up this morning! There he was, right outside my windowsill, making the strangest, most beautiful sounds I have ever heard. Boy, is he tough! He is the most magnificent grasshopper I have ever seen. Oh thank You, God! Mother said she cannot imagine how a tiny grasshopper got all the way up to my windowsill on the second floor, but we know, don't we, God? To tell the truth, he is not exactly what I had in mind for a pet, but I know he will be just perfect. I named him Chirpy because of the sound he makes. He walks up and down my arm and when I put him on the ground, he jumps right back on me again. I would like to see Timmy's fish do *that!* Chirpy crawls on my face, too. My grandmother came over today and told my Mother that Chirpy could crawl into my ear and then I would have to go to the hospital and have the doctor take him out. I had better not let Chirpy climb that far again! Good night, dear God, and thank You again. I guess You know how happy I am!

Dear God, today in class Mr. Marlow told us all about grasshoppers. Everyone agrees that I have a peculiar-looking but wonderful pet. You were smart to give Chirpy five eyes, God. He is so little he needs five eyes to warn him of danger. The two jointed "feelers" on Chirpy's head let him know how things smell and the shorter jointed "feelers" near his mouth tell him how things taste. Imagine, little antennae that smell and taste!

Mr. Marlow said that grasshoppers don't breathe through noses. Instead, they have breathing holes, called "spiracles," along each side of their bodies. They look like tiny portholes in a midget ship. And Chirpy's ears look like clear spots! Mr. Marlow made us guess where they are. (You certainly think of good hiding places, God!) We finally found Chirpy's hearing spots near his strong hind legs.

Learning about Chirpy's strange, amazing body made me appreciate him even more, God. You certainly went to a lot of trouble when you designed grasshoppers!

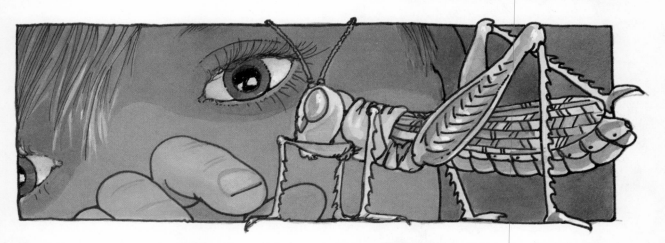

I will praise you, Lord, with all my heart; I will tell of all the wonderful things you have done.

Psalm 9:1

Ever since God created the world, his invisible qualities . . . have been clearly seen; they are perceived in the things that God has made.

Romans 1:20

Dear God, did you hear me crying tonight when Mother told me that I should let Chirpy go? She said it was cruel to keep a nice grasshopper like Chirpy in a glass jar for too long a time and that if I really loved him I would let him go. So I did. It was the hardest thing I ever had to do, harder than going to school on the first day! I know I have to mind Mother, but I love Chirpy so much.

God, please watch over Chirpy tonight like You watch over me. I put him under the little green bush near the front door, the one with the red berries on it.

I'm very sad tonight, God. But it helps to know that You care about me and about Chirpy.

Dear God, I gave my report on Chirpy this morning. Mr. Marlow said it was the first time anyone ever reported having a grasshopper for a pet. When I told Mr. Marlow that I had set Chirpy free, he said that he was sorry for me but happy for Chirpy.

I still miss him, but I guess if I were a grasshopper, I wouldn't like being kept in a jar either. I guess I'm glad that Mother told me about being kind to Chirpy.

You are my God; teach me to do your will.
Psalm 143:10

He helps us in all our troubles.
2 Corinthians 1:4

Let's Talk About This

1. Tommy had a problem. What was it?

2. What did Tommy do about his problem?

3. Do you talk to God about your problems?

4. At the end of each of Tommy's prayers is a short verse from the Bible. Each verse is about the subject of Tommy's prayer. Did you know that there are verses in the Bible about almost any problem you can think of? That is why it is so important to study the Bible; it helps

Dear God, thank You, thank You, a billion, trillion times. Chirpy is back! Like a little plane, he landed on my leg as I was leaving for school this morning. He looks better than ever. He must have eaten some good plants! Mother was right. Grasshoppers, even wonderful pet grasshoppers like Chirpy, should be free. Having Chirpy for a pet made me realize that you can love something a lot even though it is with you only a short time.

God, thank You for always being here when I need You. Once I said that Chirpy was my best friend, but, God, You are. I love You!

He is near to those who call to him.
Psalm 145:18

to know that others have felt exactly as we feel.

5. Tommy's mother said to him, "If you really love Chirpy, you will let him go." What did she mean by that? What are some other ways that we can show love to our pets?

6. When we bring an animal (or insect, or fish) into our house, it is totally dependant on us. We must give it food, a clean place to live, and time to sleep, or it will become very sick. And we should never hit our pets or be mean to them. Most pets are small and defenseless and it is just plain cruel to be mean to them. Larger pets may bite or claw us if we are mean. Why do you think some people are mean to animals?

7. Once Tommy had learned a few things about how a grasshopper is made, how did he feel about God?

8. Do you think God must be extremely smart to create all the things He's created? There is a word we use to describe how smart God is. The word is "om-ni-scient" and it means, "having *all* awareness, knowledge, and understanding." That's pretty smart, isn't it? We can use that word to describe only one being. Do you know who that is?

Mother's Not Looking

by Judy Rankin

Ding, dong. Ding, dong. Betsy ran to the front door and pulled hard to open it.

Her friend, Belinda, peeked into the living room. "Can you play?" she asked.

Betsy smiled. She had set her small table for a tea party and was hoping her friend would come by.

"We can have a tea party," she told Belinda. "I bought animal crackers and candy at the store yesterday." The girls ran to the kitchen. Betsy took the animal crackers from the cabinet. She stretched to reach the candy dish on the table. "Belinda and I want six red licorce candies," she told her mother.

Betsy's mother said, "You may each have two. If you eat too many candies and crackers, they will spoil your appetite for lunch."

The girls carried the animal crackers and candy to Betsy's tea table in the living room.

Belinda whispered to Betsy, "It's all right to get more candy when your mother's not looking."

So Betsy and Belinda crawled on hands and knees to the candy dish to get four more pieces of red licorce.

Mother peeked around the corner, smiled and said, "No more candy before lunch, Betsy."

Belinda and Betsy played dress-up in Mother's old shoes, dresses, and hats. Betsy wanted some long, black beads and perfume.

Mother said, "We don't have time to get out more things today. In just a few minutes you'll have to put away your toys and clean up. Your daddy will be home for lunch soon."

Belinda led Betsy into the play room. "We can put on perfume and jewelry while your mother's not looking," she said.

So they tiptoed to Mother's bedroom and opened her dresser drawer.

Mother's face popped into the mirror. She slowly shook her head "No."

Betsy sat on the front porch step after lunch. She watched a black blister bug crawl along the garden hose to the sprinkler. She watched a mother robin pull a long, fat worm out of the damp flower bed and flap her strong wings to carry it up to her baby birds nested in Mrs. Oliver's apple tree. Betsy wondered if mother robins told their baby birds, "No."

Betsy watched the mother robin's big dark eyes stare back at her as she flew close to the porch. The robin saw every worm that wiggled up out of the dirt. She saw Tigger Cat as he slipped around the corner of the house and crept up behind her. The mother robin could probably see everything her babies did, just as Betsy's own mother could see everything she was doing, Betsy decided.

Belinda and Thad rode their three-wheelers up the sidewalk. "Get your three wheeler and let's ride around the block." Belinda called to Betsy.

Betsy's mother was busy shining the window on the front door. "It's all right to ride on this side of the block, Betsy," she said. "But remember that you don't ride all the way around the block while the Baker baby is napping. Mrs. Baker told me that those noisy three-wheelers wake Jason up."

Belinda and Thad followed Betsy back to the garage for her three-wheeler.

"It's no fun riding up and down this side of the block." Belinda pouted. "I'm going all the way around the block. My mother doesn't care."

Betsy sat on her red three-wheeler with the fancy handlebar grips decorated with red, white, and blue streamers. It was more fun to go clear around the block, taking the corners so fast she had to lean to the inside to keep from tipping over, and feeling the breeze on her warm, sweaty face. She wanted to ride her bike fast with Belinda and Thad. Why did her mother always have to say, "No"?

"Come on, Betsy," Thad insisted. "Your mother's in the house. She won't even know you're gone."

Betsy pushed the peddles of her three-wheeler back and forth, back and forth. Maybe her mother was wrong. Maybe they could ride past Baker's house so fast that the baby would never hear them.

Maybe Belinda was right. Maybe it was all right if her mother wasn't looking.

"Let's go!" Belinda shouted.

Betsy backed her three-wheeler onto the sidewalk and peddled fast to catch up with Belinda and Thad. She rounded the corner at the side of her house so fast that the green hedge was only a fuzzy blur. She slowed down a bit to see if her mother was watching from the front porch. Betsy didn't see her. She peddled fast again. Mother wasn't looking. Belinda said it was all right if her mother wasn't looking. She could get around the block and back to her own driveway before her mother even knew she was gone.

Betsy peddled faster and faster. She caught up with Belinda and Thad at the next corner. She swung the corner behind them on two wheels, but she didn't feel the cool breeze tickling her warm face or the thrill of her heart pounding as she raced down the sidewalk.

Betsy saw the Bakers' house on down the block. She thought about baby Jason asleep in his crib. Betsy knew babies cried and fussed if they didn't finish their naps.

She slowed her three-wheeler, turned around, and slowly peddled back home.

Betsy's mother was reading her Bible on the porch. "Does any girl I know have time for cookies and lemonade?" she asked.

Betsy crashed her three-wheeler against the step to stop it and stomped up on the porch. She was angry at her mother. She didn't want dumb cookies and lemonade. She wanted to be bad and have fun with the other kids. She wanted to eat too much candy, ride where she wanted, and forget about cleaning up and being on time. She didn't want her mother always watching and telling her what to do.

Betsy plopped down in the porch swing. Her mother put a cold glass of lemonade in her hand. Betsy puffed out the pout on her mouth. The cold drops on the glass felt good to her hand, but she wouldn't drink the lemonade, she decided. She would just hold the cool glass to her hot

forehead. She was a mad, bad Betsy.

She held the glass to her cheeks, her chin. Her lips sneaked a quick sip. The lemonade felt cold and good all the way down to her tummy.

Her mother held the plate of cookies in front of her. "I don't want cookies," Betsy grouched. "I want to be bad and have fun."

Her mother looked closely at the plate of cookies. "I think this one was baked for a bad Betsy," she said, as she pointed to a cookie.

Betsy reached for the sugar cookie with red sprinkles on it. She was still angry with her mother. Maybe she wouldn't eat it. She started to put the cookie back on the plate when she heard a squawking and hissing and a flapping of wings. Betsy ran to the edge of the porch.

The mother robin swooped down and

pecked at Tigger Cat, and squawked a warning at her baby bird. The mother flew at the hissing cat again and again while the small bird hopped to safety.

Betsy jumped down from the porch and ran after Tigger Cat. "Bad cat!" she shouted. "Don't you hurt that baby bird!" She picked her cat up in her arms and carried her back to the porch swing. Betsy felt her own heart pounding inside her as she smoothed the cat's bristly fur. Her mother hugged her close.

"That baby bird was in real trouble," her mother said. "You were very brave to help the mother robin save her baby."

Betsy looked at her mother. "Do you think the mother robin told her baby not to get out of the nest?"

Betsy's mother smiled. "And the little robin thought she could try her wings when the mother wasn't looking?"

Let's Talk About This

1. Betsy's friend told her that it was OK to do things that her mother said *not* to do. Is this the kind of thing friends should tell each other? What would you do if your friend said, "It's OK to do this," when your mother told you not to do it? Would you ever tell a friend that it is OK to disobey her mother?

2. When Betsy's mother had to say "no," she told Betsy *why.* She said that six candies would spoil Betsy's lunch, she said that the girls didn't have time to get out more dress-up clothes before lunchtime, and that Betsy couldn't ride her three-wheeler around the block because the noise would wake up Jason Baker. Do you like to know *why* you can't do things? Does knowing why make it easier to obey? What made Betsy want to disobey, even though she knew there were good reasons?

3. Betsy started to disobey her mother and ride around the block anyway. She thought it would be fun to ride with the other kids, but it wasn't. Why wasn't it?

4. What do you think made Betsy stop and turn her three-wheeler around. Her mother said, "It was God talking to you today." Did she mean that Betsy actually heard God's voice?

Betsy nodded. "But you're always looking. You see everything I do."

"No, Betsy." her mother answered. "I can't see everything you do."

"Then why couldn't I ride around the block with Belinda and Thad?" Betsy asked. "I thought I came back because you were watching me."

"No, Betsy. Let me read to you from God's Word." Her mother opened the Bible. "Behold, the eye of the Lord is on those who fear Him."

"Mothers and fathers are sometimes sleepy or tired or away from their children. We cannot see everything you do, but God is with you always. It was God talking to you today."

Betsy set Tigger Cat on the floor beside her. "Then why do you always have to tell me what to do?" she asked her mother. "Why do you always say 'No'?"

"Children need mothers and fathers like Tigger Cat needs you to feed and care for him. Why did you tell Tigger 'No' just now?"

Betsy stared hard at the worn toe of her red tennis shoe.

Mother turned the pages of her Bible.

"'Children, obey your parents in the Lord, for this is what God wants you to do.' I think that little bird knows now that her mother said 'No' because she loves her," Betsy's mother told her. She kissed Betsy's pink cheeks. "I'm glad you're my Betsy!"

5. Do you know what a "conscience" is? A conscience is our understanding of what is right and wrong—it is the sense that helps us to realize when we are doing wrong. Some people call it a "voice," and say that "my conscience is speaking to me." Do you think that God can "speak" to us through our consciences? Is that what happened to Betsy?

6. When she watched the mother bird attack Tigger Cat, Betsy realized that the mother was trying to protect her baby. Then she thought about the times when her own mother said, "no." What did Betsy realize—what did she begin to see that her mother was trying to do?

7. Our parents make rules for us and tell us what we can and cannot do because they love us and are trying to protect us. Why do you think God makes rules for all of us—young and old? Why is one of God's rules, "obey your parents"?

8. If rules are made to protect us and help us lead happier lives, we should be thankful for rules, shouldn't we? If rules are made because God and our parents love us and care very much about what happens to us, rules should remind us that we are loved. What do you think about that—how does it make you feel?

Furlin's Forgiveness

by Kathleen M. Shaffer

Meet Furlin, the squirrel.

Now, most squirrels spend their days running, and jumping, and climbing trees in the thick of the woods to gather nuts and berries for food—but not Furlin.

Furlin was a lazy squirrel. He would just lie in his nest in the poplar tree, with his tail wrapped around himself for a blanket, and sleep away the hours in the sunshine. Instead of working during the daytime like the rest of the squirrels, he would go out at night and take away *their* nuts to eat for himself.

"This is really easy!" Furlin would think. At night while the squirrel families were fast asleep, he would sneak to their trees without a chatter. Up to their nests

he would climb, using his tail to balance himself. Carefully he would pick out the nuts, especially acorns, his favorite. Furlin was so quiet that no one discovered it until morning.

"Oh, no! This is terrible!" shrieked Rina the red squirrel when she woke up to find that her nut pile was gone. "We will have no food for the winter!"

Her two little ones cried and cried.

"I'm going to catch the thief!" shouted Sunny, their father.

Later that morning Sunny and some of his neighbors, whose winter supply had also been robbed, got together to figure out how to catch the thief.

First they tried to trap him in a pool of sticky tree sap.

But that didn't work. As soon as Furlin got close to the branch dripping with sap, he smelled it. With one superb spring of his hind legs, he soared over their trap.

Then they tried stringing empty nut shells and acorn tops all around the tree, so that the thief would make noise when he came to steal the food.

But Furlin just carefully climbed across each string and didn't rattle any nuts.

"I'm having even more fun, now!" he chuckled to himself. It was exciting for him to see if he could outwit all the other squirrels, dodge every trap, and still get their nuts.

And he did!

Sunny and his neighbors got angrier and ANGRIER! Each day they put their ideas together to invent newer and more clever traps. But there was one squirrel in the woods who would not join them. Her name was Sesame.

Sesame the Squirrel was quiet and gentle. She felt sorry for the nut-thief, in a way, wondering if he were lonely or hungry. So, instead of putting out a trap for Furlin, she wrote him a note one night, and put it by the pile of food stored in her nest.

"Take plenty," the note said, "I gathered extra for you.—Sesame"

That night Furlin crept silently up her tree and peeked into her nest. He grabbed the letter, but almost could not believe his eyes when he read it!

"Why would someone write something like this?" Furlin marveled.

He was so confused that he scampered speedily home, even forgetting to take the nuts he had come to get.

All day and all night long Furlin sat and thought about Sesame's letter.

"She would do that for me?" he wondered, "I'm just a rotten squirrel that steals everyone else's nuts!" He felt so bad that tears squeezed out of his eyes. He didn't know what to do.

Then Furlin began to think, "I should just work in the daytime, like all the other squirrels in the woods. Then maybe they'd be my friends.

23

"I could even pay them back for the nuts I took by giving them a big party!"

So Furlin got up very early each morning, even before the sun, to scurry and scout for the best nuts, mushrooms, flowers, and berries in the woods.

"This will make a fine feast for my friends!" he squeaked. The pile was so big, there was hardly room in his nest to sleep.

"It's time to send out the invitations," Furlin decided, "I'll write:
'Come to *Furlin's Feast* tomorrow, at my nest in the poplar tree.
                    See you there.
                    Furlin'"

Soon everyone was chit-chattering excitedly about Furlin's big party.

All the squirrels in the woods came to Furlin's house the next day. Even Sesame was there.

And what a delicious banquet they had! They danced and played until they couldn't anymore.

Furlin never had such a good time.

All too soon it was time to say goodbye.

"Wait a minute, everyone!" Furlin shouted, "I-I have something to say to you." He gulped and looked down at his paws.

"I must apologize to all of you," he spoke softly, "I'm the one you've tried to catch every night—I'm the nut-thief."

Not one sound was heard.

"But I promise that I will never do it again—and I hope you will all forgive me and be my friends."

After a moment, Sesame got up and kissed Furlin on the cheek. "Of course we will!" she laughed.

Soon everyone came closer to shake Furlin's paw, or hug him, or kiss him. "You've more than made up for your bad deeds," they said, "If *you* try, we'll try to be your friends."

And Furlin did.

Every day he got up bright and early with the sun to gather food for himself. Furlin worked so fast that he even had time left over to help the other squirrel families rebuild their winter supplies.

Never again did Furlin steal anyone else's nuts. And never were all the squirrels in the woods ever so happy!

Let's Talk About This

1. The story says Furlin was lazy. Do you know what lazy means? Hint: Furlin would rather sleep than work.

2. Furlin did not gather nuts. How did he get food to eat? What do we call someone who takes things that belong to others?

3. Do you think Furlin meant to hurt any of the other squirrels? Or was he just goofing around, without thinking?

4. What would happen to the squirrels during the winter if they didn't have any nuts saved up? This makes what Furlin was doing much worse, doesn't it? Have you ever done something thinking it was just a little bit wrong, and found out later that it caused a terrible problem?

5. One of the very neatest things about God's Word is that it tells us if we will sometimes do just the opposite of what we *feel* like doing, things will turn out better. Here is an example. When people do mean things to you, and make you cry or make you angry, you may feel like doing mean things to them. But the Bible tells you to do something *nice* for the person who hurt you. Isn't that what Sesame did for Furlin? How did Sesame's letter make Furlin feel? Can you think why he felt that way? If you did something nice for someone who was mean to you, do you think he might stop and think about what he had done to you?

6. Furlin was sorry for being selfish and lazy, so what did he decide to do? At the party, what did Furlin say to all the other squirrels? Not only that he was sorry, but that he would never ____? Is this a good way to fix things when you've done something wrong?

7. After Furlin admitted that he was the thief, said he was sorry, and that he'd never steal nuts again, what did the other squirrels say to him? The Bible calls this "forgiving." Forgiving is part of fixing a mistake too—if others don't forgive you when you say you're sorry, is the problem really over?

8. We may think we can make someone feel bad if we don't forgive him when he says he's sorry, but life doesn't work that way. God says *you* are supposed to apologize when you hurt someone, and *you* are supposed to forgive someone who has hurt you. If you don't forgive, you are the one who feels bad, not the person who has already apologized. Why do you suppose God arranged things like that?

GOD CARES ABOUT MY FAMILY

The Sister Switch

by Linda L. Hall

A little girl named Cricket Bowers lived with her big sister named Button Bowers. Button was much bigger than Cricket, two whole years bigger. Button was seven years old, and Cricket was only five. When Cricket was really little, she thought she would grow as big as Button. But every time Cricket got bigger, so did Button.

Cricket and Button had long, proper names too. Cricket's birth certificate said Carolyn Elizabeth Bowers, and Button's said Barbara Joan Bowers. Everyone liked to call them by their nicknames instead.

Daddy had nicknamed Carolyn "Cricket" because of her tiny arms and legs that flew all over the place when she ran. Mother had nicknamed Barbara "Button" because of her big round eyes. Cricket thought her nickname was just for a little girl, and she liked Button's nickname better.

Everything about Button was a lot more special than Cricket, Cricket thought. Button was bigger and prettier and got to do everything there was to do. People were always telling Cricket, "Wait until you're a little older, like Button. You'll get your turn."

One Saturday morning Cricket decided that she couldn't wait for her turn any longer. She didn't want to be Cricket anymore, or Carolyn Elizabeth, either. She wanted to be Button.

All week long, Button had done exciting things. On Monday her friend Judy invited her to go roller skating after school. Tuesday she went to her Brownie-Scout meeting. Wednesday she celebrated her friend Mandy's birthday. And Thursday she stayed overnight at her friend Erin's house and went to school with her the next morning.

All week long Cricket said, "I don't have anything to do." All week Cricket's mother said, "You have puzzles and games and books and so many things to play with. I played by myself sometimes when I was a little girl, and I enjoyed it."

Cricket's week was extra sad because she didn't even have anybody to stand in the school-bus line with. Her kindergarten friend Lucy had to stay home because she had the measles. Cricket felt very lonely even though she lived with a mother, a daddy, and a sister. None of them understood why she got tears in her eyes all the time and wanted to cry.

So, of course, when Carolyn Elizabeth woke up on Saturday morning, she wanted to be Barbara Joan instead.

"I'm going to be Button today," she announced at breakfast.

"You can't be me," Button stated matter-of-factly as she scooped cereal into her mouth. "I'm already me."

"I can be you if I want to, and I want to," retorted Cricket. "What kind of cereal are you eating? I'm going to eat it too."

"If you're me, who will I be?" asked Button angrily.

"Oh, you can still be you. I'm just going to be you too," Cricket replied cheerfully.

Mother and Daddy looked at each other with a "This-is-going-to-be-one-of-those-days" look on their faces.

"We'll miss Cricket," joked Daddy.

"Don't you girls fight," warned Mother.

After breakfast Cricket and Button went upstairs to make Button's bed. Cricket's side of the room looked real sloppy because there was no Cricket to clean it up today.

Button dressed in a pair of shorts, so Cricket put on a pair of Button's shorts too. Only on Cricket they weren't very short and they surely weren't very comfortable, either.

Then Button trotted next door to get her friend Kerry so that they could work on their sticker collections. Cricket really wanted to roller skate. But if Button wanted to work on stickers, Cricket would play stickers too. She got her mother's grocery stamps out of the kitchen drawer and pasted them on pieces of notebook paper.

"Why is Cricket tagging along with us?" asked Kerry.

"Oh, it's alright, she just wants to pretend she's me today," said Button.

When lunchtime came, Button and Kerry were playing school on Kerry's patio, and Cricket was very bored. Still, she had to keep being Button. Kerry's mother came out on the patio and asked, "Would you like to stay for lunch, Button? Oh, Cricket, I didn't know you were here also. You're welcome to stay if you like."

"I'm Button today," Cricket corrected her.

"Well, then, Button, Button, and Kerry, come in for lunch."

When Cricket saw the tuna fish salad Kerry's mother had made, with all the little pieces of things like celery floating in it, she felt a twinge about being Button. Her own mother knew that she didn't like tuna fish. If she were at home being herself, she could talk her mother into letting her eat a peanut butter sandwich and a banana.

Kerry went shopping with her mother after lunch. Cricket and Button wandered back to their own house. They saw Daddy getting into the car.

"Hi, girls," called Daddy. "I'm going to the store to buy something for Mother's lamp. Do you want to come with me?"

"No, I want to stay home," said Button. She never liked to go on errands.

"Then I can't go, either," said Cricket. "I'm Button today. Remember?"

"Oh, that's right," said Daddy. He looked a little disappointed. "Well OK, I'll see you later."

Cricket loved to go on errands with Daddy. He still held her hand, just like he did when she was three and four years old. She couldn't admit it to anyone, but she still liked having her hand held.

Daddy also swung her up onto counters at stores so she could see everything that was going on. He even pointed out the things that he wanted on the different shelves so that Cricket could pick them up. Five years old wasn't quite too old for those things, but seven definitely was. "I bet Daddy would have gotten me a little treat," thought Cricket sadly, "since Button got to do so many things this week and I didn't get to do any."

Cricket and Button sat down on their front steps to think about what they should do next. The Singleton sisters were walking down the street and they were also looking for something to do. Sissy Singleton was Button's age, and Sally was Cricket's age.

Sissy asked Button if she would like to practice the stitching that they were learning in Brownie Scouts. Sally asked Cricket if she would like to ride bikes.

"I'm Button today," said Cricket, "so I have to do what Button does."

"How come?" asked Sally.

"Because Button has all the fun, and I want to be her."

"OK," said Sally, and she went to look for someone else to play with.

Cricket surely couldn't see the fun of sewing special sit-upon cushions for Brownie Scouts; but if Button was doing it, it had to be fun, didn't it?

Right now Cricket couldn't imagine sitting upon anything at all because Button's shorts felt so uncomfortable. And to think she could be wearing her own favorite pink pair with the butterfly embroidered on the pocket.

When Button and Sissy got tired of working on their sit-upons, they decided to pick daisies and chant a song. As they plucked off petals, they recited, "He loves me, he loves me not," about the boys they liked at school. Cricket didn't like any of the boys in her class, but today she was Button so she had to pick daisies anyway.

By dinner time, Cricket decided she hadn't had a very fun day at all. If she had been herself instead of Button, she would have roller skated and biked and hop-scotched and gotten dirty. Stickers and sit-upons and daisies and playing school weren't good at all for Saturdays.

Grandpa came to Cricket and Button's house for dinner. After he kissed Button, he asked, "Where's my little Cricket? I want to throw her into the air."

"I'm Button today," Cricket said with a tear in her eye. "You have to give me just a little kiss on the cheek because that's what Button likes."

"Nobody to throw into the air today," Grandpa sighed with disappointment. "I love my big Button, but I certainly do miss my little Cricket."

"I miss her too," said Daddy. "Errands were lonely for me today."

"I miss Cricket also," said Mother. "Both my girls are special to me. I wanted two daughters, not just one. And I wanted them to be different, not the same."

"I miss my sister," said Button.

"You do?" asked Cricket, surprised.

"Well, sure," said Button, "it's no fun having two of me. I need a sister."

"I just get jealous sometimes," Cricket admitted ashamedly. "You can do so many things because you are bigger than I am. And besides, you even have a nicer nickname because of your pretty eyes."

"That's funny," Button said, puzzled. "Lots of times I wish I were younger because young kids get spoiled. And your nickname is Cricket because you almost fly when you run. I wish I could run that fast."

"Sounds to me like we all have things to be thankful for," Grandpa reminded them.

"You know," said Cricket thoughtfully, "I didn't really like being Button after all. I have a lot more fun being me. I guess I am pretty important and special, aren't I?"

"We're certainly glad you figured that out," Mother smiled. "And you know who is most glad of all? God is."

"Yes," continued Daddy, "because God made you like nobody else. He doesn't want you to be anybody but yourself. That's how important you are to Him."

"Wow!" exclaimed Cricket. "I'd never want to make God sad. I'm happy God made me. I'm happy He made us all. I like being me, and from now on, I'm *always* going to be Carolyn Elizabeth Cricket Bowers!"

Let's Talk About This

1. Have you ever wished that you could be someone else? Have you ever wanted to be exactly like someone else?

2. Think about all the different people you know—friends, relatives, the girl at the grocery checkout, the man at the gas station. What would your life be like if all these people were the same?

3. Think of some people you know whom you are always very happy to see. What makes these people special? If everyone was the same, would anyone be special?

4. Cricket was sad because Button got to do things that Cricket wasn't allowed or wasn't able to do. Have you ever felt like that? Can you think of some things that you are able to do this year that you couldn't do last year?

5. Instead of being sad about things you are not yet able to do, why not be happy about how much you have already grown, and look forward to when you grow some more and get to do even more things?

6. There will always be people who can do things that you cannot, even when you are an adult. This is because God made us to be different, and have different abilities. There will also be ways in which you are special, and can do things that others cannot. Learn to be thankful for these differences instead of letting them make you sad.

A Little Baby With a Big Problem

by Carolyn S. Tauzel

Do you know what the word "handicapped" means? I didn't until a few years ago. Then something happened that made my whole family learn a lot about people who have handicaps. There are many different kind of handicaps. The one I want to tell you about is a hearing handicap. That means that the handicapped person's ears do not work well, and he has trouble hearing sounds. If the handicap is very bad, the person cannot hear at all. Let me tell you how I happened to learn all of this.

My name is Patti Griffin. I'm nine years old, and I'm in the third grade. I live in a big house with my mother and dad. We have a large back yard with three dogs and a lot of toys. We are very happy, but there is something I want very much.

I was five years old when I said, "Mother, could I have a baby brother or sister? I could play with the baby. I could talk to him. I could sing songs to him. I could even help you take care of him—or her! It would be so much fun."

"You're right," said Mother. "It would be fun to have a baby in the house."

That night I asked God to please send us a new baby. Every night after that I remembered to ask God for a baby brother or sister for me to play with and help take care of.

I was so excited I could hardly stand it when I found out a few months later that I really was going to get a baby brother or sister! I could hardly wait. But I had to wait several more months while the baby was getting ready to be born.

Finally the day came. My baby brother was born, and Dad took me to the hospital to see him. There, behind a glass window, was a tiny baby with a sign on his bassinette that said "GRIFFIN," so I knew that he was our baby. He was so small and so cute. Dad said he was perfect in every way—just like I'd been when I was born. We decided to name our new baby Norman. Dad and I thanked God right then and there for giving us such a wonderful baby boy.

Mother and Norman came home from the hospital later that week. I was very excited to have them home. I sat beside Norman's crib for hours telling him about all sorts of things. When he cried, I sang my favorite Sunday-school songs to him—I think "Jesus Loves Me" was his favorite. It was lots of fun to have a baby at home. We were all very happy.

On Norman's first birthday, we had a big party. My Grandpa and Grandma Griffin, my Grandma Wilson, and Aunt Trudy and Uncle Max, and Aunt Lucy and Uncle Bob all came. We had cake and ice cream. We played games and had a wonderful time. Then I heard one of my aunts say something that bothered me. "He seems so smart. I wonder why he isn't talking yet? He's awfully quiet for a one-year-old.

"Mother," I asked her later that day, "why doesn't Norman talk yet? I heard

Aunt Lucy say that he's very quiet for his age. Is there something wrong with him?"

Mother looked very sad when she answered me. "Patti, your daddy and I have been watching Norman lately. Aunt Lucy was right. He *is* very quiet. We've noticed other things, too. Most babies get scared when they hear loud sounds. Norman doesn't even notice them. He doesn't notice music on the radio. When I walk up behind Norman, he doesn't seem to know I'm there until he sees me. Your daddy and I are wondering if Norman is having trouble with his hearing."

"But Mother, how will we find out if he can hear?" I asked.

"I've made an appointment to take your brother to audiologist. Audiologists work with people who have hearing handicaps," said Mother.

"Hearing *what?*" I asked.

"Handicaps," Mother answered. "A person who has a handicap has a part of his or her body that did not develop right. Or perhaps an accident or an illness caused the damage. Whatever the reason, a handicap makes it hard for that person to use the damaged part of his or her body. If the handicap is severe, the body part cannot be used at all. People with hearing handicaps find it hard to talk and learn because they cannot hear what is being said and they do not know how words sound. If a hearing handicap is so severe that the person cannot hear at all, we say that the person is 'deaf.' Some deaf people and most people with limited hearing can learn to talk, but they need the help of a special teacher called a 'therapist.' If Norman has a hearing handicap, he will need the help of a therapist and we'll need to work with him in a special way to teach him things."

"But why did God send us a baby with a handicap?" I asked.

"We don't always understand why things happen as they do," Mother replied, "but you can be sure that God will help us to do whatever we need to do for Norman, and God will help Norman live with his handicap."

Norman went to see the audiologist. Sure enough, he was having a lot of trouble hearing. In fact, he was having so much trouble that he started wearing a hearing aid. Dr. Bennett, the audiologist, told us that the hearing aid would make sounds louder so that Norman could hear them. The hearing aid looked a little strange at first, sticking out of Norman's ear, but now I'm used to it and don't even notice it.

A speech therapist started teaching Norman to talk. She showed us how to help him too. My special job is to show Norman pictures and tell him what they are. I make sure he watches my mouth when I say the words. He's learned all kinds of new words. He's even beginning to say the words after me too. It's fun playing school with him.

At first I felt weird having a brother who was handicapped. I was afraid that meant he would act funny and people would laugh at him. I was wrong, though. Norman's very smart. There are all kinds of things he can do. Everybody thinks he's terrific and so do I.

Norman will be three years old soon. You know, Mother was right. God has helped us learn and do all sorts of different things. Helping Norman has helped me too. I have learned lots of things by working with him. Who knows? Maybe I'll work with hearing handicapped children when I grow up.

I still don't know *why* God let Norman be handicapped. But I'm glad he's my brother. I think Norman is the best brother God could have ever given me. I don't even think of him as handicapped any more—just different in a special way.

Let's Talk About This

1. Turn the volume off on your television set and watch a program for five minutes. How did you feel while you were "hearing handicapped"?

2. How would you feel if you had to wear a hearing aid all the time? Would you worry about what other people thought?

3. Ask someone who wears a hearing aid what things are hard for him to do and understand.

4. Try to imagine how difficult it would be to learn new things if you could not hear. What would you do in school? This is why there are special schools for people with handicaps—not because they aren't just as smart as you, but because they need special help to get the information in the first place.

5. What other situations (besides school) would be very difficult for someone who could not hear? What sorts of things would a deaf person be unable to enjoy?

6. In the story, Patti said that she made sure Norman was watching her mouth when she was teaching him to talk. Why? What does this let you know that you should do when talking to a person who is "hard of hearing"?

7. What other ways could you help people who are hearing handicapped? How would you explain an emergency to them? How could you give them some difficult directions?

8. Should we feel sorry for people who are handicapped? Does the fact that some people are *not* handicapped make them better than handicapped people?

9. Do you think that God can use handicapped people to do great things? Do you think that God loves handicapped people as much as unhandicapped people?

10. If God loves everybody just the same, how should we love everybody?

Did You Hear Me, God?

by Barbara Lockwood

Kevin could hardly wait until his birthday. His Mother and Dad asked him to write a "Wish List," and at the top of it he wrote in big, bold letters: POCKET KNIFE. In fact, he also wrote that on a list he mailed to his Uncle Bill and his grandmother.

At last there were only four days until his birthday. All Kevin thought about and talked about was his knife. "If I had a knife, I could help you fix dinner," he assured his mother. "I could save you lots of time—you wouldn't have to stand here so long and chop the vegetables."

After dinner that night Kevin saw his father stacking a pile of old newspapers in the garage. The Boy Scout paper drive was this Saturday. "If I had a pocket knife, I could cut that string for you, Dad," he suggested to his father, who was tying a string around the bundle of papers.

Kevin wondered if anyone was going to buy him a knife. He remembered his birthday last year. He had asked for a gun, but got a truck instead.

In Kevin's Sunday-school class the teacher taught the children all about prayer and how God cares about our needs and answers our prayers. They even sang a song called "God Answers Prayer."

So, Kevin decided he'd better pray about the knife he wanted so badly. "God, please let my mother and dad get me that pocket knife I saw at the store. I want the shiny, red one, with a can opener. Oh, and thanks."

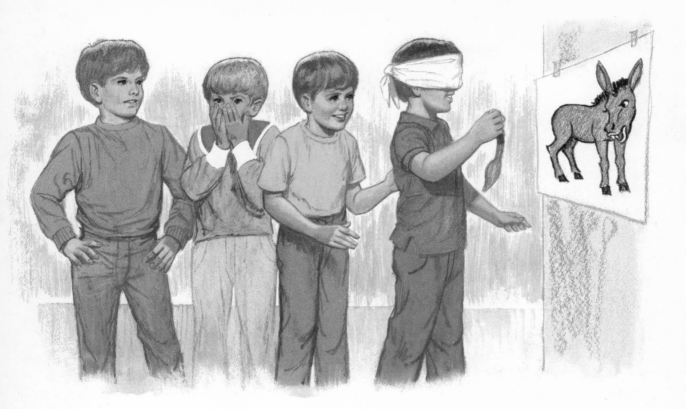

Kevin's birthday finally came. Nick, Timmy, Barry, and Gabriel arrived right on time. Jason was the only one who didn't show up.

It was a great party. Kevin's mother hid prizes around the yard and the boys all went on a treasure hunt. Then they played "Pin the Tail on the Donkey." After the games they all sat at the picnic table in the backyard to watch Kevin open his presents.

Kevin looked through the pile for the smallest package. Hoping it was the pocket knife, he ripped off the paper and hurriedly opened the box. No, It wasn't a knife, but a Mickey Mouse watch. "Thanks, Barry," he mumbled as he stuffed the watch back in the box.

He opened the next smallest box, but it was a race car from Gabriel. Timmy's gift to Kevin was a set of felt pens, and Nick gave him a magic kit. No knife yet. Kevin then opened the gifts from his parents, and the ones that arrived in the mail from his Uncle Bill and his grandma. Still no pocket knife. He was glad to get the new toys, but he just could not stop thinking about that knife.

I'm angry with You, God, Kevin thought. *I thought You answered the prayers of kids who love You. And You know I do,* he pouted to himself.

As Kevin's mother carried out the birthday cake, the boys began to sing "Happy Birthday." The cake was a huge, gray robot with M&M's for the mouth and eyes, and chocolate donuts for the wheels. Before he blew out the candles Kevin closed his eyes and wished again, as hard as he could, for the knife. He blew out the candles in one big breath, and his mother cut a piece for each person. It was chocolate under the frosting and tasted yummy with the peppermint-stick ice cream. The ice

41

cream was cold and sweet as it slid down their throats on that hot, summer afternoon.

After playing with Kevin's new toys for a while, the boys began to leave. As they left they thanked Kevin for inviting them to his party. Kevin closed the door and went to the living room to watch T.V. "I wonder why Jason didn't come?" he thought as he flopped down on the couch.

A few minutes later the doorbell rang. "I'll get it," Kevin yelled to his mother as he ran to the door. When he opened the door he was surprised to see Jason standing on the porch, staring at the floor. Jason had a present in one hand and a funny looking bandage on the other.

"I'm sorry I had to miss your party," he said sadly as he looked up at Kevin. "Here's your present." Kevin stared at the bandaged hand. "Thanks," he replied, "but what's that thing on your hand?"

"That's why I had to miss your party," Jason answered softly. "I was at the doctor's office getting stitches." Jason hung his head, staring at the floor again. "I was

in my dad's workshop and found his pocket knife. I was trying to make a boat, ya see, and the dumb ol' knife slipped and cut my hand. It bled like crazy, and boy, did it ever hurt!"

Jason's mother was honking the horn, signaling for him to come back to the car. "Bye," he said as he turned to leave. "Hope ya had a nice party."

"Thanks for the gift," Kevin yelled as he waved good-bye to Jason and shut the door. "Who was that?" asked Kevin's mother as she came in from the kitchen. "It was Jason," he answered. Kevin told his mother the reason Jason didn't come to the party.

"Honey," she said as she sat Kevin down on the couch next to her and held his hands, "that's why your father and I didn't buy you a knife for your birthday. You and Jason are the same age and we just don't feel that you are old enough for something so dangerous."

"But I prayed, and Jesus didn't answer my prayer," he whined. "I just guess He doesn't care about me."

"Kevin, God does care about you. He loves you very much. But sometimes God answers our prayers with a 'no.' He does answer each and every prayer, but He knows what's best for us and because He loves us so much He wants what is best for us. Sometimes that means He must say no."

Kevin thought about that for a minute. "I guess I should apologize for getting so mad at Him," he finally said. So Kevin prayed, "Jesus, I guess You knew what was the best thing for me when You answered my prayer with a 'no.' I guess You're right—I'm not old enough yet to have my own pocket knife. Sorry I got so angry with You. Oh—and thanks for answering my prayer."

Let's Talk About This

1. Kevin wanted the knife very much. He told several people exactly which knife he wanted and he even prayed to God about it. But did he get the knife?

2. Kevin's mother explained to him why she did not buy the knife. What did she say?

3. Kevin's mother doesn't like to disappoint him, but more importantly, she doesn't want Kevin to accidentally cut himself. Can you see that she said "no" *because* she loves Kevin?

4. God sometime says "no" for the same reason. God knows that sometimes, what we think will bring us happiness will bring us sorrow instead, so He says, "no." This is a very hard lesson. Even some adults think that God's "no" means He is unhappy with them, or doesn't love them anymore. Is this true?

5. The Bible tells us that God loves all of us, all the time. We can't "earn" His love by being good, because He already loves us—whether we are good or not. So if God ever answers one of your prayers by saying "no," remember that He still loves you, and may be saying "no" to protect you.

6. Since God loves us no matter how we act, does this mean He doesn't care how we act? Your parents are disappointed when you misbehave, but they still love you. Is God the same way? When you know that you have hurt your parents by doing something wrong, do you also hurt? Do we hurt God when we are bad?

43

Grandpa's Swing

by Patty Hayman

Grandpa's swing was Kelli's favorite place. It wasn't that the swing itself was so special. It was old, needed paint, and squeaked with every backward motion. It wasn't even a very comfortable place to sit. But for as long as Kelli could remember, the swing had been Grandpa and Kelli's private talking place. That is why it was so special.

Kelli's mother was going to have a baby soon, so Kelli and Grandpa were talking about the names the family had considered as they sat on the swing one day.

"How about Jonathan Troy?" Kelli asked.

"Hmmm. That one sounds pretty good to me," Grandpa answered.

"I like it too, if the baby is a boy," said Kelli. "Now, if it's a girl. . . ."

"If it's a girl," Grandpa finished, "I just hope she has the same beautiful smile as her older sister!"

Kelli laughed and kissed Grandpa on his cheek. It was warm and soft with wrinkles.

A month ago Grandpa had an operation. Kelli didn't know much about it, except that it had something to do with cancer. Kelli's mother had explained that the disease called cancer was filling Grandpa's body. Since his operation, too much activity would make Grandpa tired. Kelli could see that he was beginning to nod his head now. He would be taking his nap soon.

"Would you like having a glass of milk, Grandpa?" she asked carefully.

"Not now," he whispered, leaning back in the swing and closing his eyes. "Why don't you let me rest awhile?"

"OK," Kelli answered. "I'll go see how Mother's doing with the wallpaper. Call me if you want anything."

Grandpa didn't answer.

Upstairs, the baby's room was looking more complete. Kelli's own baby bed had been refinished and decorated with Winnie-the-Pooh decals. Now, Mother was covering the walls with baby-print wallpaper.

As Kelli entered the room, she offered to help. Mother accepted gladly. She showed Kelli how to measure, paste, and hand her a strip of wallpaper. Kelli liked the way Mother depended on her now, since Dad was away on a business trip.

"What's Grandpa doing?" Mother asked, smoothing a strip of paper.

"Oh, he's resting on the swing. He wanted me to leave him alone for a while." There was an ache in Kelli's voice. Grandpa had always loved her company before, but not lately.

"Kelli," Mother began, "I know that sometimes Grandpa doesn't seem to be the same. But he still loves you—all of us—very much. We've got to try to understand how he feels, and to keep on loving him, the way he is now, and the way he may become."

Kelli understood. The doctors said they had done all that they could do for Grandpa. They didn't have much hope that Grandpa would get any better, only worse. Yet, Kelli secretly hoped that one day soon she would be able to help Grandpa forget his illness, and make him smile again.

Mother went on. "It's hard for me to see Grandpa this way too. But remember, the Lord is with us to help us, if we will ask Him. 'God is our refuge and strength, a very present help in trouble.'"

Kelli loved to hear Mother quote verses from the Bible. It seemed she had a verse in her head for any situation. There was strength in those words. They made Kelli feel better.

A week passed quickly. Grandpa spent most of his time resting on the sofa, or sitting in his swing. Although Kelli tried to interest him in other things, he didn't want to play games with her, or make cookies, or watch television. He didn't even go to church with them on Sunday morning.

On Thursday evening, when Grandpa suggested that Kelli go along with Mother to her baby shower, Kelli leaned back to study Grandpa's face. He looked tired. He seemed far away. He wasn't even looking at her.

Kelli decided that he needed to be alone again. "OK," she said. "I'll go, and I'll bring you a piece of the cake."

The baby shower was more fun than Kelli expected. After the games, Mother opened her gifts while Kelli enjoyed nuts, mints, cake, and punch. Still, she found herself thinking about Grandpa and won-dering what he was doing. Then she re-membered she had promised to bring him a piece of cake. She hopped from her seat and carefully chose a big piece with lots of frosting. She wrapped the cake, plate and all, with a napkin and returned to her seat.

The gifts Mother had opened were now spread on top of a table for all to see. Kelli thought, "Soon our house will look like that—baby things everywhere. It will be nice to have a baby around, especially since Grandpa is so sick." She checked the wrapping on Grandpa's cake. Grandpa had always been her best friend. She hated to think that things were changing between them. It just didn't seem right. Did God know what He was doing?

Kelli thought of the verse Mother had quoted for her. She quietly prayed, "God, please be my helper. And please take care of Grandpa too."

Kelli and Mother got home late. As they pulled in the driveway, Mother said, "I had better check on Grandpa. Why don't you start carrying in these gifts for me?" Kelli nodded.

Kelli found that if she stacked the boxes, she could carry five or six at a time. She was making her last trip into the house as Mother came down the stairs. Mother was crying.

"Something has happened to Grandpa," Mother whispered. "We need to call an ambulance." She hurried to the phone in the kitchen.

Kelli stood frozen for a moment. Then she was frightened and thought *What do you mean? What has happened to Grandpa?*

She ran upstairs. Grandpa's room was dark. He lay motionless in bed.

"Grandpa?" she called from the door-way. "I brought you some cake!" Grandpa didn't answer. "Remember, I promised to bring you some cake?"

Grandpa didn't answer, couldn't answer.

The ambulance came within minutes and took Grandpa to the hospital. But there was nothing the doctors could do to help him. Grandpa died, Mother said, because of the cancer. The cancer just got to be too much for him.

Driving home from the hospital, Mother explained, "Grandpa is with Jesus now, Kelli. Jesus said, 'I am the resurrection and the life; he who believes in Me shall live even if he dies.'"

The next couple of days were filled with phone calls, cards and letters, flowers, visits from the minister and others, and tears. Lots of them, sometimes.

Dad cut his business trip short and flew home in time for Grandpa's funeral. Kelli

47

was scared. She was glad Dad was home.

The funeral was held in the church building. It was filled with flowers. Grandpa was in a long box called a casket, covered up to his waist with a blanket. His head was on a pillow. He looked like he was sleeping. A lady sang a song and some people cried, even though it was a happy song about Jesus and Heaven. Then the minister stood to speak. His message was not like a regular sermon. He read from the Bible, but then he talked about Grandpa. The pastor said many nice things about him. Kelli felt better after he spoke.

Next, everyone did something Kelli didn't expect. One by one, the people went to Grandpa, looked at him for a moment, then moved on. When Kelli's turn came, she squeezed Dad's hand so she wouldn't have to go alone. Dad stood with her. Neither one of them said a word. Kelli thought that maybe she had seen Grandpa move his fingers a little earlier. She checked. No, he wasn't moving at all. She and her dad went on.

All the people went to their cars. Grandpa's casket was put into the back of a big car called a hearse. All the other cars followed the hearse to the cemetery. Again, the minister spoke, with everyone gathered around the closed casket. This time Kelli held Mother's hand, not because Kelli needed it, but because Mother did.

Three days later, things were finally getting back to normal. Most of Grandpa's things had been packed up or given away. But no one even talked about getting rid of Grandpa's swing. Kelli was glad.

That night, right after supper, Mother began having pains. The baby was coming! As they had planned, Mother and

Dad took Kelli to stay overnight with Mrs. Grayson, before going on to the hospital.

Kelli fidgeted most of the evening. Mrs. Grayson offered to play a game, but Kelli wasn't interested.

"Things happen so fast," Kelli said. Mrs. Grayson listened. "I miss my grandpa. Missing him still hurts, but right now, all I can think about is the new baby, and that makes me happy."

"I understand," Mrs. Grayson began. "When you lose someone you love, it is very painful. The part of you that is your grandpa's granddaughter is hurting. You will miss him for a long time. But God has a way of making it better for you. He needs you to be a sister to a new baby, and that's a joyful thing. You don't have to feel bad about being happy and sad at the same time."

Kelli and Mrs. Grayson knelt together before Kelli went to bed to thank God for His care, and to ask Him to help Mother and Dad and the new baby.

A phone call came at about 6:30 the next morning. It was Dad.

"It's a boy!" he said. "You have a baby brother!"

And for the first time since Grandpa died, Kelli understood that the sadness would slip away and make room for happiness to flow in.

Mother and the baby, Jonathan Troy, had to stay in the hospital for a couple of days, so that evening Kelli and Dad were alone, sitting together on Grandpa's swing.

"Do you think Grandpa knows about Jonathan?" Kelli asked.

Dad paused, then said, "I don't know. I believe that the Lord is celebrating tonight and perhaps Grandpa knows about Jonathan's birth too."

Kelli thought about that for a moment, then jumped up quickly. "I'll be back in a minute," she called. When she returned, she was carrying a paper plate, wrapped in a napkin, and two forks.

"This was supposed to be for Grandpa," she began, unwrapping the cake, "but I'm sure he won't mind if we eat it. We need to celebrate, too. After all, today is Jonathan's birthday!"

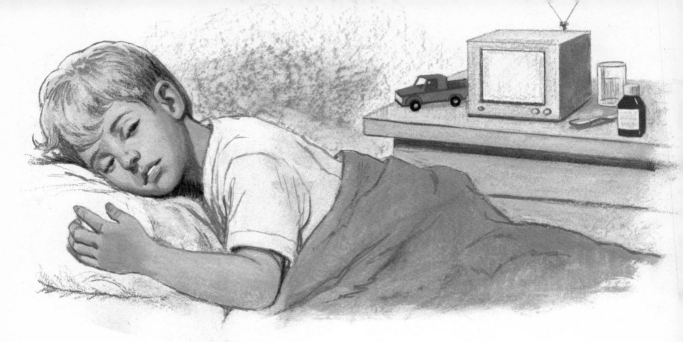

Let's Talk About This

1. When Grandpa was very sick, he didn't feel like having Kelli around. Do you think he wanted to feel like that? Did it mean that he didn't love Kelli anymore?

2. When Grandpa died, his body was buried in a cemetery. Later, Kelli's Mother said that Grandpa was with Jesus. How could this be?

3. The Bible promises us that when a Christian dies, he or she will go to live with God. Even though we may not know exactly *when* this happens, it still is very comforting to know. Many people actually look forward to dying, so that they can be with God. Why then do we cry when someone dies? Kelli was sad that her Grandpa was no longer with her. But do you suppose that she could have been happier if she had thought about Grandpa being with God, and not being sick anymore? (The Bible also promises us that there will be no sickness in Heaven, and no one will ever cry.)

4. Have you ever been so sick that you didn't care about doing anything? Does this help you to understand how Grandpa felt? Will it help you to understand the next time your Mother has a very bad headache, or your dad has an awful cold?

5. When Grandpa died, people talked about the nice things they remembered about him. Why? If someone you loved died, would it make you feel better to think about when he or she was happy and well?

6. Kelli's baby brother was born just after her Grandpa died. Someday, Kelli's mother and dad will die, and Kelli will die, and Jonathan will die. This is natural and we should not be afraid of death, because the Bible promises that there is life after death for those who love God. How can you know what God wants you do do? If you study God's Word, and try your very best to obey it, will there be any reason for you to be afraid to die?

A
Special
Baby

by Carolyn S. Tauzel

Hi! My name is Scott. I'm going to tell you a story about my neighbors, Mr. and Mrs. Cain. Something wonderful just happened at their house!

Mr. and Mrs. Cain are a nice couple. Mr. Cain works with my dad, and Mrs. Cain teaches second grade at my school. They live in a big house with two dogs and a cat. They go to our church and they're lots of fun.

One day, a long time ago, I asked Mrs. Cain why she didn't have any children. She told me that she and her husband wanted to have a child, and that they hoped God would send them a baby soon. Later, I heard Mrs. Cain tell Mother about an appointment she had made. She and her husband were going to talk to a lady at an adoption agency. When she left, I asked Mother what an adoption agency was.

"An adoption agency," she told me, "is a place that helps babies find a home with loving parents. The people who work in the agency find a special couple like Mr. and Mrs. Cain to become the parents of one of these babies."

"But why don't Mr. and Mrs. Cain just go to the hospital like everyone else?" I asked. "That's where other parents get their babies."

"Do you remember learning in Sunday school that God works to make every-thing turn out in the best possible way?" Mother asked me. "Maybe God saw that one of the babies at the adoption agency will need special parents like Mr. and Mrs. Cain. Whatever the reason, Mr. and Mrs. Cain are sure that God will sent them a very special baby through the adoption agency."

That night when I said my prayers, I asked God to help Mr. and Mrs. Cain find the perfect baby for them.

Then one day I saw a pretty lady drive into the Cain's driveway. Mrs. Cain told me later that the lady is a social worker, and her name is Mrs. Donnelly. She was the person from the adoption agency who was helping them find their baby. I got so excited that I started making plans! I decided what toys I could bring over for the baby. I talked about taking the baby for walks. I had all kinds of things to do with the new baby.

"Don't get too excited just yet," Mrs. Cain laughed. "It may take quite a while for Mrs. Donnelly to find the right baby for us. We need to be patient. One thing we can do is keep asking God to help her."

So we waited and we prayed. One day, Mother and Dad got my old crib out of the attic and took it to the Cain's house. "Is the baby there yet?" I asked. "Not yet," said Mother. "Just be patient."

I saw Mr. Cain walk into his house the next day with a stroller and a baby swing. "Is the baby there yet?" I called. "Not yet," he said. "Just be patient."

A few days later Mrs. Cain showed Mother lots of new baby clothes. "Is the baby there *yet?*" I asked. "Not yet," said Mrs. Cain. "Just be patient."

It's hard to be patient when you're waiting for a new baby to move in! I went to school and did all my homework. I played with my friends. I went to Sunday school and church. I kept a close eye on the Cain house, though. I didn't want the new baby to move in without my knowing it! I even said lots of prayers that God would send a baby to the Cain's very soon.

One Saturday, Mother woke me up early. "We've been invited to the Cain's house for lunch today," she said with a twinkle in her eye. "They've invited another little boy that they think you'll enjoy meeting."

We went to the Cain's house at lunchtime. I didn't see another boy there so I decided he must be late. I sat by the window and watched for a little boy to come.

"Where is he?" I asked Mr. Cain.

"He overslept, but he'll be here in a little while," Mr. Cain told me.

"What's his name?" I asked.

"His name is Robert," Mr. Cain answered.

"How old is he? Does he go to my school? What does he like to play?" I asked.

"Now just hold on," laughed Mr. Cain.

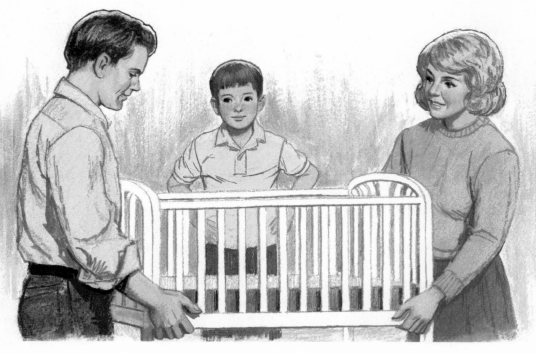

weeks old. He won't go to school for quite a while. You may help us find out what he likes to play," she said with a smile. "So what do you think of your new friend?"

Well, I think that this is the most terrific thing that's happened in our neighborhood for a long time! And tonight when I say my prayers, I'm going to thank God for sending that special baby to that special family and for letting me be his special friend.

"He's too young to go to school. I haven't asked him what he likes to play. You'll meet him soon, though. Then you can ask him yourself."

I waited and waited and *waited.* Still no Robert!

"Scott!" Mother called. "Robert's in the kitchen waiting for you!"

What?" I thought. *I hadn't seen him come in!* I went to the kitchen to see how he'd sneaked in without seeing him. Mother, Dad, and Mr. Cain were standing there smiling. In a chair sat Mrs. Cain holding a tiny baby boy!

"Scott," Mrs. Cain said. "We'd like you to meet Robert Cain. He's three

Let's Talk About This

1. Have you ever known any families who adopted a baby? If so, how did they act as they waited for the new baby to arrive?

2. As the story said, God works to make things turn out in the best possible way. Why do you think God sends some children to their homes through an adoption agency?

3. Do you know anyone who is adopted? Ask that person how he or she feels about being adopted.

4. Do you think parents love their children differently if they are adopted than if they were born to them? Ask parents who have adopted a child how they feel about this question.

5. How would you feel if you found out you were adopted? Would it make you feel different in a funny way or different in a special way? Or would it make you feel different at all?

The Boy Who Wanted to Be King

by Marjorie Hodgson Parker

Philip peeked into his grandfather's tent. "Grandpa!" he whispered. The old shepherd woke and blinked at Philip in the early morning light. "Zuki is gone again."

"That troublesome goat," Grandpa grumbled. "She is more trouble than a whole flock of sheep and goats. Someone who finds her is sure to make a goatskin out of her." He got up. "And it may be me," he added.

"Oh, Grandpa," Philip sighed. "She is just curious. We can look for her on our way to Bethlehem. You wanted to get an early start before the registration line gets too long. Remember?"

"Yes," Grandfather recalled, pulling on his sandals for their walk into their hometown of Bethlehem, the City of David. "I'm sure I'll be in line most of the day."

Already the road was getting crowded. The emperor's census was filling the roads with caravans. "Grandfather, look at the rich man and his camels!" Philip pointed. "I'll bet Bethlehem hasn't seen anyone that important since King David!"

Grandfather smiled. "That may be, Son. But someday, our Savior the Messiah will be born there. That will be a far greater honor."

Philip was hardly listening. He was watching the crowds and looking for Zuki. "Grandpa," he cried suddenly. "I'll bet I know where Zuki is! Since she thinks

she is a person, she is probably standing in line in town to register."

They both laughed. Grandfather shook his head. "You have spoiled that nanny goat," he said. "She prefers people to animals and parched wheat treats to grass." As he said this, he handed Philip a snack of parched wheat and also a fig cake his Aunt Miriam had made.

"That's it, Grandpa! Zuke is looking for something good to eat. I'll bet she has gone to the innkeeper's stable. She loved the sweet hay there."

Last week the innkeeper, an old friend, had asked Grandpa to build a wooden feeding trough, a manger, for his donkey and ox. Inside the limestone cave that was used as the innkeeper's stable, Grandpa had labored while Zuki ate her fill of hay. Philip had watched Grandpa's knotty old fingers make a strong manger and even carve a star on the side of it.

"Grandpa," Philip said now as he ate his fig cake, "Why did you spend so long on that manger? Nobody cares what a dumb old manger looks like."

"Whatever my hand finds to do, I do it with all my might," Grandfather said, smiling.

"But that manger is fit for a king!" Philip said. He felt almost angry that his grandfather just wasted his talent. He could have been a respected artisan, wearing a chip of wood behind his ear to set him apart. But, instead, he had chosen to be a poor shepherd. And he gave away everything he made.

"Grandpa, why do you work so hard for nothing?" Philip asked.

"I get something," his grandfather answered, ruffing up Philip's brown hair. "I get enjoyment doing things for people. And with just a little extra effort, I can make something ordinary into something special."

"But who cares about a special manger? Nobody sees it!" Philip persisted.

"I care. God sees it. Now run on and see if you can find Zuki before she gets into trouble. Remember when she broke Aunt Miriam's water pot? A stranger would *eat* your goat for that. Hurry! I'll meet you at the square."

Philip's heart raced as fast as his feet. Surely no one would eat *Zuki!* As he entered the village he saw Aunt Miriam on her flat rooftop, hanging out clothes. "Have you seen Zuki?" he called.

"I tried to catch that bad nanny," she answered. "Look! I made her a collar." She tossed the woven collar down to Philip and wagged a finger at him. "Maybe that will help you keep her out of trouble. Zuki ran away from me and headed toward the inn."

"Thank you, Aunt Miriam!" Philip called. So Zuki *was* at the stable. He ran to the cave. Sure enough! Zuki lay next to the donkey. She scrambled to her feet, glad to see Philip.

"Zuki, you bad girl!" he scolded gently, rubbing her floppy brown and white ears. "Why do you get into so much mischief? You are no ordinary goat, that's for sure!"

He knew how Zuki felt. He didn't want to be ordinary, either. Being a shepherd wasn't so bad, but he would rather be a king. And why not? The shepherd David had become a king.

He slipped Aunt Miriam's little collar over Zuki's head and held tight as he led her to the crowded square. Grandpa registered, then they walked back to the hillside to watch the flocks.

At evening, Grandpa lit a fire and other

shepherds joined them, bringing wine-skins and cheese. They told stories around the fire. "Tell about David and Goliath, Grandpa," Philip begged.

"Always King David!" Grandpa complained. "All right, my boy, but remember, you don't have to be a king or slay giants to be special to God."

"But I want to be chosen by God like King David was—for something special."

"You are special to God just the way you are, Lad. Take what He has given you to do and make the most of it."

"Like you did with the manger?"

The old man smiled and nodded. Philip leaned against his grandfather and looked toward the heavens. Why did Grandpa think that with all those stars up there, God would notice one more small star? Especially one carved into the side of a manger?

As Grandfather began telling the familiar story, Philip felt very sleepy. Much later, he thought he was dreaming when he heard a stranger's voice.

He sat up. There was such brightness it was like daytime. "Grandfather!" he whispered. He was afraid.

Grandpa was sitting up straight, his mouth hanging open. Zuki hid her head against Philip. The other shepherds didn't move. They looked terrified too.

From the brightness came an angel's voice, saying, "Be not afraid; for behold, I bring you good news of a great joy which will come to all people; for to you is born this day in the City of David a Savior, who is Christ the Lord. And this will be a sign for you: You will find a babe wrapped in swaddling clothes and lying in a manger."

Philip's heart was pounding in his ears. And then more angels joined the first and they praised God. Philip held on tightly to his grandfather and stared in wonder. Was he dreaming?

Then, suddenly, the angels were gone. No one moved. The shepherds looked at one another in amazement. Grandpa whispered, "Let's go to Bethlehem and see this wonderful thing that the Lord has made known to us."

Philip slid his hand back into his grandfather's as they walked. He didn't know which of them was trembling most. Even Zuki pressed close as they hurried toward Bethlehem.

Bethlehem was quiet. No one else knew the wonderful news! Suddenly, Zuki dashed ahead, right around the hill to the innkeeper's stable. Did she know something, or was she just being naughty again? Philip tried to catch her. The goat stopped at the cave's entrance. The shepherds caught up with her.

Inside, a lighted lamp cast a golden glow over a young couple and a baby who was wrapped in swaddling clothes. And lying in a manger! Just as the angel had said.

Philip fell on his knees alongside the others. "The Messiah!" he breathed. He

and the other shepherds had been chosen to know God's Good News first. And here they were! Not kings or wealthy people, but lowly shepherds.

And then Philip noticed. The baby was lying in the manger Grandpa had so carefully carved. With a star on it—fit for a king.

"Oh, Grandpa," Philip whispered. "God did see your work! He has honored the labor of your hands!"

His grandfather's gnarled hands were clasped prayerfully. Tears streaked his cheeks. "God has honored us all," he said quietly.

Philip pulled Zuki close to him. She, too, was shivering with excitement. "Now I know how David felt," he whispered to her. "And I feel like a king too!"

Let's Talk About This

1. The author of this story has imagined some events that might have taken place around the birth of Jesus. It is OK to imagine that a boy named Philip visited the stable when Jesus was born, but we should be careful not to get our imaginary stories mixed up with the real reports in the Bible.

2. According to this story, Philip and his grandfather were going to Bethlehem for the same reason that Joseph and Mary were going. What reason was that?

3. Philip was a little upset with his grandfather. Why?

4. He thought that his grandfather could be a great woodcrafter, and that he was wasting his time on little jobs and by being a shepherd. How did Grandfather explain to Philip that he was not wasting his time?

5. Have you ever felt that your jobs at home are unimportant? Stop and imagine what your house would be like if you didn't do your jobs.

6. Grandpa told Philip that he took great care with simple jobs because, "whatever my hand finds to do, I do it with all my might." He was quoting King Solomon, perhaps the wisest man who ever lived, whose writings are recorded in the Bible. The teaching that Grandpa was quoting is found in Ecclesiastes 9:10. Since Solomon lived long before Jesus was born, his writings would have been known by anyone who studied the Scriptures. We know from our story that Philip and his grandfather had studied the Scriptures because Philip talked about the shepherd boy, David, who had become king, and Grandpa talked about the Savior Messiah who would one day be born in Bethlehem. The story of David is found in 1 Samuel, and the prophecies concerning the coming Messiah (Jesus) are found all through the Old Testament Scriptures.

So Grandpa knew it was important to do a good job on every job, because of what Solomon said. We know it from Solomon *and* because of what the Apostle Paul said (Colossians 3:17), "And whatever you do, whether in word or deed, do it all in the name of the Lord Jesus, giving thanks to God the Father through him." What does this verse mean? Do you think that if you remembered this verse each time you had a job to do that you would have a good attitude about the job?

7. At the close of the story, Grandpa says to Philip, "God has honored us all." What did he mean—how has God honored us?

8. We are thankful to God because He loved us enough to honor us by sending Jesus to save us. Philip learned one way to show his thankfulness. What is that way?

Piper

by Marjorie Hodgson Parker

Piper squinted at the bright sunlight dancing on the Sea of Galilee. He waved to his father, who was leaning against one of the wooden boats pulled up on the beach. Father was talking with other fishermen as they mended their nets. But Andrew was not among them. Where was he? Piper had hoped to see him today. But Andrew wasn't around much since

he'd met that man named Jesus.

Piper pulled up his tunic and waded into the Sea of Galilee. He held the small net Andrew had given him. Even though Andrew was a grown man, he was Piper's friend. Andrew liked listening to Piper play the flute as they mended fishing nets on the beach. The reed flute was how Piper got his nickname. He liked to pipe

tunes on it, and always carried it in his belt.

Piper scooped the net through the water. He fished a long time but caught only two little ones. He tossed them into his basket on the beach.

"Ha, ha, ha!" boomed a voice behind him.

"Hello, Josh," Piper said, even before he looked around. He recognized Josh's unkind laugh.

Josh was a tall, strong boy, but not much older than Piper. Piper wanted to be his friend, but Josh didn't act like a friend. "Scrawny little fish for a scrawny little kid," Josh teased, swinging on the limb of a myrtle tree near the water.

Piper felt his face flush. "I've got to go. I have to help my father." He pulled himself up as tall as he could when he passed Josh. But he knew stretching didn't help much.

"You'd better stick to mending nets," Josh laughed. "You'll never make a fisherman. A bigger fish would have pulled *you* in!"

Piper pulled out his flute. He hoped music would drown out Josh's words. But he heard them anyway. "Too bad you can't race with us this afternoon, Kid!" Josh called. "But since you won't be there, someone else will have the chance to come in last!"

Piper dug his toes into the warm sand. His basket bumped against him in time to the music he piped, and in his head he sang:

"If I could have a wish come true,
    I'd wish that I were tall.
I could do big things, yes, sir,
    If I were not so small."

Piper didn't see Andrew. "Hello, little Piper," Andrew said, patting Piper's head with a big hand. He peeked at Piper's fish. "So you tried out the net. Good! Those little fish should make just the right sized lunch for you."

Piper was almost ashamed of the fish. He hated their littleness. He hated *being* little.

"Where have you been, Andrew?" Piper asked.

"With Jesus," he answered. "I have become a fisher of men."

Piper laughed. "You'd need a really big net to catch men!"

"It sounds funny, I know," Andrew smiled. "But Jesus is teaching me and my brother, Simon Peter, and others how to catch men for God. You have heard of the

Messiah, haven't you, Piper? Well, He is here! Jesus is the Messiah, God's Son. And I am one of His followers."

"Isn't Jesus the carpenter who does magic?" Piper asked. He had heard of Jesus making crippled men walk and blind men see.

"He is a carpenter, but His works are miracles, not magic. He is more than a healer though; come and hear Him one day. He often teaches around here."

"I'll come," Piper answered. He wanted to meet Jesus. He had a special miracle he wanted Him to do.

Since his father didn't need him to work, Piper started walking home. He played another tune on his flute, and in his head he sang:

"Since Jesus is the Son of God,
   I'll ask Him one fine day:
'Sir, will you kindly make me big?'
   And this is what He'll say:
'Yes, you can win the races
   And catch the biggest fish.
I will make you tall and strong,
   Because that is your wish.'"

Many days later, Piper's mother gave him a small basket of lunch and said, "I pickled the two fish you caught."

He thanked her, but he didn't feel very thankful. Those dumb fish! He had almost forgotten them. Now they looked even smaller next to the five barley loaves his mother had also put in his basket.

He hugged her good-bye, then walked toward the beach with his father.

"Andrew told me Jesus will be here today," his father said. "I can't go hear him, but you may, if you'd like."

"Oh, yes!" Piper cried.

"Andrew said you can tell where Jesus is by the crowds." He pointed toward the beach. "And there they are."

"I'd better go catch them. 'Bye, Father," he cried as he ran.

"Listen well. And don't stay too late!" his father called. Piper waved.

Piper had never seen so many people. Maybe there were thousands! But he couldn't see Andrew or Jesus.

Piper was breathing hard when the crowd finally slowed at the top of a rocky, grass-covered hill. He knew Jesus must be nearby, but he couldn't see over peoples' heads. *If only I were tall!* he thought. He squeezed through the mob, trying to catch a glimpse of Jesus. He heard cries of "I can walk!" and "Glory to God!" Piper pushed through the bodies blocking him. He *had* to get through to see.

He bumped into someone—someone with big sandals that were facing his. Piper was afraid to look up, but the figure wouldn't move. So he had to glance upward. Andrew!

"Would you like to see Jesus?" Andrew asked, easily swinging Piper up to his shoulders. From there Piper could see. And there was Jesus! He was bending over a man who was lying down. He touched him and said something. The man jumped to his feet and shouted with joy.

"I see Him!" Piper shouted. "Jesus just healed a crippled man!"

"Yes, lad," Andrew smiled as he put Piper down. "I'm glad you came. And I'm glad you brought your lunch, because it looks like Jesus will be here all day. I must go. Listen well."

As the crowd parted for Andrew, Piper saw Josh. Josh looked jealous. Josh hadn't gotten to see Jesus like Piper had. Piper walked over to him.

"It's a good thing you have a big friend, Runt," Josh growled. "Even *I* can't see. But I don't care much about seeing Jesus, anyway. I'm just looking forward to eating. Look." He pulled a huge smoked fish from his bag. "And I have some date and raisin cakes too."

Piper's mouth watered, but he said, "Shhh. Jesus is talking." He strained to hear. The crowd grew quiet and Piper heard Jesus' voice, strong and clear. Jesus told about God and explained Scriptures. His words were like nothing Piper had ever heard.

Before he knew it, it was evening. Piper's stomach rumbled and reminded him he hadn't eaten. He noticed Josh hadn't eaten yet, either. Suddenly, Andrew stood beside them again.

"Jesus needs food to feed this hungry crowd, Piper," Andrew told him.

"He can have my loaves and fishes!" Piper offered happily. Then he remembered how small the fish were and felt silly. "But it's not much."

Josh didn't offer his big fish. Instead, he said, "You won't feed many people with *those* fish." Piper felt embarrassed. But Andrew took the basket and thanked him, then disappeared into the crowd.

People began sitting down. At last Piper could see! He watched Jesus take his mother's barley loaves and break them into bite sizes and give thanks for them. He did the same with the little fish. And then, Jesus looked right at him. Piper had never seen such love in someone's eyes— not even his mother's!

Andrew and the other disciples began passing around Piper's bread and fish. Baskets full! How could Jesus make so much out of so little? When a basket came by Piper and Josh, they looked at each other in amazement. Piper ate some. It was delicious!

Then, when everyone had eaten, Andrew and the others collected leftovers. Twelve baskets full! Piper could hardly believe the miracle that had happened right in front of him. He heard people exclaim, "This is surely the Prophet who was to come into the world."

Still dazed, Piper realized it was late. He threaded his way through clumps of people, then ran toward home. It didn't matter now how small he was, he felt ten feet tall! He wanted to shout! Jesus had used *his* fish and his loaves!

"Wait, Piper!" he heard Josh call. "Piper!" Josh had called him *Piper* and not Runt or Kid. Josh walked alongside him, silent for once.

When they passed a beggar by the road, Josh stopped. He reached in his sack and pulled out the fish he'd forgotten to eat. He gave it to the beggar. And the cakes too. Piper smiled.

Piper took out his flute and played the happiest tune he could think of. It even made Josh laugh. Then Piper danced a little jig around his friend as he sang the words in his head:
"I was a part of a miracle
  On a hill in Galilee.
Jesus fed thousands with my small fish!
  Think what He can do with me!"

Let's Talk About This

1. The real story about the boy who gave his lunch to Jesus is found in Matthew 14:13-21 and John 6:1-14. The story of "Piper" is what this author imagines might have happened. We don't know for sure that Jesus' disciple Andrew was a friend of a boy named Piper, but he might have been. It is OK to imagine what things might have been like for the people we read about in the Bible, as long as we don't get our ideas mixed up with what is really true.

2. In the beginning of the story, Piper was unhappy about something—something that Josh teased him about. What was it?

3. Piper thought that if he ever met Jesus, he would ask Jesus to make him taller. But when he did meet Jesus, he forgot all about being taller. What made him forget?

4. Jesus performed a miracle using Piper's lunch. What was the miracle? Why was Jesus able to do something like this? To whom did Jesus give thanks for the bread and the fish?

5. Andrew explained to Piper that Jesus performed miracles—not magic. What is the difference?

6. Josh had been mean to Piper and called him names, but after the boys heard Jesus speak, Josh was kind to Piper and to a beggar they passed on their way home. What caused Josh to change?

7. On the way home Piper "felt ten feet tall." Why did he feel so good about himself then? He also said, "It doesn't matter how small you are, if you feel tall inside." What does that mean?

8. Read Piper's very last song again—it explains exactly why Piper was so happy and so excited about the future. What was true for Piper is true for us, too. God can do anything. We may sometimes feel like we are small and unimportant, but God can use us to do wonderful things. How does that fact make you feel? The next time someone is mean to you and you start to feel sad, remember that you are very important to God, and that God loves you very much. Will you still feel sad?

Long ago, Jacob, who was also called Israel, was chosen by God to be the leader of all his family members, who were then called Israelites. God loved the Israelites very much, and took care of them in a special way. About 450 years after Jacob (or Israel) died, his people had grown into a very large nation. But they had become slaves to the people in Egypt. The Israelites were slaves for a long, long time, and their lives were very hard.

One day, God chose a man named Moses from all other Israelites to do a special job. The job was leading the people of Israel (the children of Jacob) from the country of Egypt, to a country called Canaan. The Israelites knew that Canaan was the most beautiful country in all the world. Because God had promised that one day they would live there, they called it "The Promised Land."

Egypt was ruled by a cruel king who hated God and God's special people, the Israelites. The King of Egypt was called Pharaoh.

The day that God called Moses to do this special job, Moses was in the desert. He tended sheep and goats and made sure they had plenty of green grass to eat and fresh water to drink.

The desert was very large and Moses drove his flock of sheep and goats from one side of the desert to the other. Moses thought he had seen everything there was to see in the desert, but on this day, he saw something he had never seen before.

Moses had just found a good place for his flock to graze when he saw a burning bush. Now it may not have been too strange to see a bush burning in the desert, for the desert is hot and dry. But *this* burning bush was strange because it didn't burn up!

Yes, You Can, Moses!

by Sandra Brooks

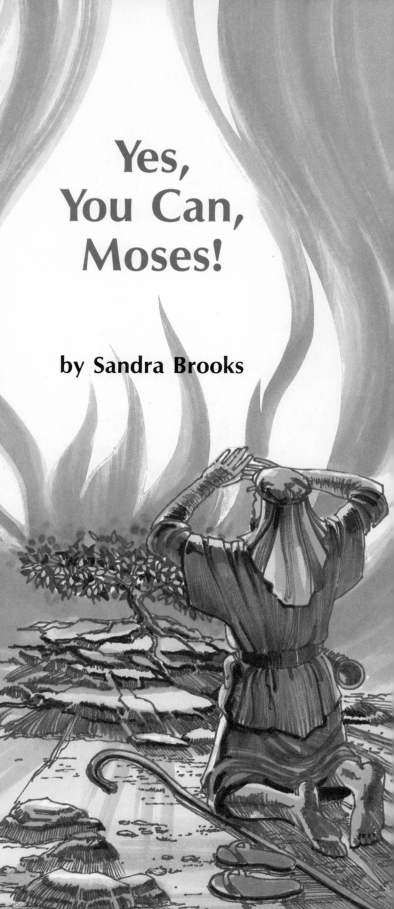

Moses came closer to the bush to get a
better look. Then Moses heard a voice.
"Moses! Moses! Listen to Me.
I AM GOD."
Moses hid his face. He was afraid.

Then God said, "I have seen how unhappy my people are in Egypt and I want you to bring them home to Canaan. I want you to go to Pharaoh and tell him to let my people go."

"I can't, God," said Moses. "I'm not important enough for Pharaoh to listen to me. I just can't do it."

But God said, "Yes, you can, Moses. I will go with you and help you. All you have to do is follow me and do what I say."

"But, God," said Moses, "what will I say? You know I stutter and can't think of the right things to say."

But God said, "Yes, you can, Moses. I will go with you and help you. You must follow me and do what I say."

Then Moses said, "O Lord, please get someone else. I can't do this thing!"

"Yes, you can, Moses. I told you I'd go with you, but if you feel you need someone else, I'll send your brother Aaron with you."

Then Moses agreed, even though he still didn't believe he could do what God wanted.

Moses went to Pharaoh and asked him to let the people of Israel go.

Pharaoh said, "NO!" And he was so angry that he punished the people of Israel.

"I told You I couldn't do this job, God," said Moses.

But God said, "Yes, you can, Moses. I told you I would help you. Now go to Pharaoh again."

And Moses did go back . . . again, and again, and again.
And each time Pharaoh said "no." But God punished Pharaoh and the Egyptian people for Pharaoh's stubbornness.

The tenth time Pharaoh refused to free the Israelites, God punished the Egyptians so severely that Pharaoh said, "Get these people out of here! They have caused us enough trouble. We'll even pay them to go!"

After the Israelites started home, Pharaoh changed his mind. He called his army and chased them to the Red Sea.

The people of Israel saw the Egyptians coming. They were afraid, and so was Moses.

Moses said, "See, God, I told you I couldn't do this thing. Now we're trapped. Pharaoh will surely kill us all! The Egyptians are behind us, and we can't get across the sea, because we have no boats."

But God said, "Yes, you can, Moses. I told you I am with you and will help you. Now stretch out your hand over the sea."

Moses did as God said, and right before his eyes, God split open the water and held it back to make a dry path across the bottom of the sea. When all the Israelites were safely on the other side, the Egyptians tried to follow, and God turned loose the water and drowned them all.

This true story of how God helped Moses and the Israelites teaches us about God's great power and His love for His people. It shows us that God will help us to do whatever we have to do.

Sometimes we have to do things that seem too hard for us, like learning to swim or taking out the garbage or telling the truth, even when it means getting punished.

But, no matter what we have to do, or what is bothering us, we can trust God to help. If we obey God and keep trying to do our best, we can do anything God wants us to. He goes with us and helps us every step of the way.

Let's Talk About This

1. Perhaps you already knew the story about Moses—or you can read in Exodus 3—14 about how God spoke to Moses through a burning bush, gave him the power to perform miracles in Egypt, and then parted the water in the Red Sea so that Moses and the Israelites could get to the other side. But did you ever stop to think about how frightened Moses must have been?

2. Even though God actually talked to Moses and Moses knew without a doubt how powerful *God* is, Moses was just a regular man, and he was afraid to go to the mighty and cruel Pharaoh and ask that the Israelites be set free. Have you ever been afraid to ask your Mother or dad for something? How would you feel if someone told you to go to the President of the United States, or the Queen of England, and ask for some really big favor that would cost a lot of money? Do you think that even your mother and dad would be afraid to ask a favor from somebody so important?

3. God helped Moses by telling him what to say, and what miracles to perform, and by giving him courage. God helps us in similar ways when we ask Him to. He gives us the courage to do frightening things (like telling mother that we accidentally broke her favorite vase). Courage is sometimes called "strength." God gives us the *strength* to do difficult things (like being kind to the person who told the lie that got you in trouble). What are some other times when you might be afraid or tempted to be angry, when you could ask God for help?

4. You might think that Moses was a very important man, and that is why God chose him for such a big job. The truth is that Moses was just a regular man who *became* important *because* God chose him, and because Moses obeyed. Each of us is just as important to God and He can use us if we will also be obedient.

5. God may never ask you to speak to a king or save a nation—but He might! He may ask you to be a missionary doctor, or an electrical engineer, or a scientist. While you are young, God asks you to obey your parents, be kind to others, and learn about Him. Whatever God asks you to do, even if it seems very, very hard, God will help you to do it. How does this fact make you feel?

73

You're Not Alone, Elijah

by Sandra Brooks

Elijah was getting angrier and angrier. He was angry about what King Ahab and his wife Jezebel were doing.

Elijah had been God's prophet in Israel for many years. A prophet is something like a preacher. He tells the people what God wants them to know.

Jezebel had made a god from a piece of wood and she named it Baal. She talked to it and bowed down to it just as if it were the real God.

Jezebel wanted Baal to be just like God. Because God has prophets, she chose 450 prophets to speak for Baal. Then she ordered the people of Israel to worship Baal instead of the real God.

One day Elijah told Ahab and Jezebel that God hated what they were doing. He told them there would be no more rain to make the food grow or to provide water to drink because they were bowing down to that silly piece of wood. This made Ahab and Jezebel very angry. They wanted to kill Elijah, but God hid him and kept him safe.

Almost three years passed without any rain. Then God said, "Elijah, go back to Ahab and tell him that now I will send rain." Ahab blamed Elijah for the fact that there had been no rain for three years. He was very angry at Elijah and wanted to kill him. But Elijah knew that God was using him and would protect him, so he went to Ahab and said, "It is time for the people to decide whether the Lord is God, or Baal is God, so let's give them a a chance to decide."

Elijah told Ahab to call the people from all over Israel. He asked Ahab, Baal's 450 prophets, and the people to meet him on Mt. Carmel.

When everyone got to the mountaintop, Elijah said, "You build an altar to Baal, and I will build an altar to God. Then we will offer a sacrifice. Baal's prophets will call upon their god to burn their sacrifice, and I will call upon my God to burn my sacrifice. The God who answers will be the God of Israel, and the people will serve Him only."

All the people and prophets agreed and the contest began.

For most of the day Baal's prophets sang and they danced and they shouted LOUDER! and LOUDER!

But there was no answer.

Elijah just sat chuckling at them and making fun of them. "Why don't you shout a little louder?" he teased. "Maybe he's too busy to answer right now, or maybe he's taking a nap!"

Finally, Elijah said, "Can't you see that Baal isn't going to answer? Now come over here and I'll show you what a *real* God can do."

Elijah built the Lord's altar and dug a deep ditch around it. Then he placed a sacrifice on the altar and told the people to pour enough water over the sacrifice to make the ditch run over. This would surely show the people how powerful God is. *And then Elijah prayed.*

Instantly! Lightning flashed from Heaven, burned up the sacrifice, and dried up ALL the water!

Then all the people fell to the ground and worshiped the Lord, the one true God.

Elijah took all of Baal's prophets and killed them. Now they couldn't lie to the people anymore. They couldn't pretend Baal was God.

And Elijah prayed again, and it rained and it rained and it rained.

When Jezebel heard what happened on Mt. Carmel, she flew into a rage. She vowed to kill Elijah before another day passed. When Elijah heard this, he became afraid. He couldn't understand. How could the people let Jezebel do this to him after what they had seen what God could do on Mt. Carmel?

How could God let Jezebel do this to him after he had done all God told him? Elijah felt alone. AND HE RAN!

Running into the desert as fast and as far as he could, Elijah was worn out.

He lay down under a juniper tree and said sorrowfully, "Lord, just let me die." Then he fell fast asleep.

Elijah felt sorry for himself. He should have known that God had protected him from Jezebel before, as He would again. Elijah just wasn't thinking clearly. He was very tired from everything that had happened and he needed some food and rest. God sent an angel to take care of him.

After a while, God sent the angel to wake Elijah and send him on his way.

When Elijah came to a mountain in a place called Horeb, he hid in a cave.

God came to Elijah and asked, "What are you doing here, Elijah?"

Elijah answered, "I worked very hard for you, God. I did all you told me, but the people have rejected *You* and *me.*

Ahab and Jezebel have killed all your prophets except me. I'm all alone."

"You're not alone, Elijah," said God. Seven thousand other people in Israel have never worshiped Baal. Even if there weren't seven thousand others, I am with you. You're never alone."

Elijah knew what God said was true. He returned to Israel and finished his job.

Sometimes we feel all alone, when we lose a pet, or our best friend moves away, or it seems like there is no one to play with us. But there are people all around us who feel just as lonely as we do. We just don't know about them.

When we feel lonely, we can pray for God to send us new friends. But the best part is . . .

. . . even when there are no friends around, God is. He never, never leaves us alone. We can talk to Him and tell Him things we can't tell anyone else, because He loves us and cares for us more than anyone else can.

Let's Talk About This

1. Elijah was another man, like Moses, who did some very brave things because God asked him to, and God helped him. You can read about Elijah in 1 Kings, chapters eighteen and nineteen. But even though Elijah had been very brave, what did he do when he heard that Queen Jezebel wanted to kill him?

2. God had already protected Elijah from Ahab and Jezebel, and Elijah had already seen God's mighty power when He sent the lightning to burn up the sopping wet sacrifice. Elijah *knew* how powerful God is, but he became afraid anyway. We call that "losing faith in God." That doesn't mean that Elijah lost *all* his faith and never found it again, it means that he lost it for a little while—he forgot to concentrate on how strong God is and worried instead about how weak he was. Do you ever do that?

3. We are like Elijah. Sometimes we are brave and other times we are full of fear. Did God get angry with Elijah when he ran and hid? What did God do for Elijah? Does God stop loving us when we worry about things instead of asking Him for help?

4. Faith is a funny thing because the more you use it, the more you have; and the less you use it, the less you have. Children often have more faith than adults because children haven't yet learned to be afraid. Right now, while you are young, you *know* that God loves you and you *trust* Him to take care of you. But sometimes, grown-ups get so frightened of grown-up things that they forget about how easy it is to trust God. Then they have to learn all over again, and as they trust God to take care of little problems, their faith grows a little bit. As they trust God to take care of bigger problems, their faith gets bigger. Finally, their faith is big and strong and allows God to do great things in their lives. Do you think you can always trust God? Will you remember when you are scared that God can take care of much bigger problems than the ones you have? Will you trust God to take care of all your problems, so that your faith can grow to be big and strong?

77

God Is On Your Side

Noah was a special man. He built a boat so large that it took many years to build. The people in his town laughed at him because there weren't any rivers or oceans nearby to float the boat. When Noah finished the boat, it began to rain. It rained for forty days and nights until water covered the entire earth!

But Noah wasn't scared during the flood. Do you know why? Because God was on his side!

Moses was a special man. God told him to go help his people. Moses led all his people out of Egypt. When they came to the Red Sea, they didn't know how to get across the water. Moses asked God to help them and the waters opened up so Moses and his people could pass through.

As Moses walked between the two giant walls of water, he wasn't afraid! Do you know why? Because God was on his side!

Paul was a special man. He was the first missionary. Paul would go from town to town telling the people about Jesus. Some of the people didn't like Paul. They would beat him and throw rocks at him. Finally, Paul was arrested and sent to a prison in Rome. Even while Paul was a prisoner, he told everybody about Jesus.

And Paul wasn't scared in prison! Do you know why? Because God was on his side!

You are a very special person too! God loves you so much that He let His Son, Jesus, die on the cross so that you can live with Him in Heaven someday. So, if you ever go to a far away country like Africa or India, or you just stay right in your hometown, you never need to be scared to tell people about Jesus!

Do you know why? Because God is on your side!

by Roger Vance

79

Let's Talk About This

1. The Bible tells us about many people, like Noah, Moses, and Paul, who were able to do great things for God because they trusted Him and turned to Him for help. Why do you think God saved all these stories in His Word for us? How do you feel when you hear the stories? Do they make you want to trust God too?

2. Noah, Moses, and Paul *were* special men, but they were first ordinary men. What made them special was that they loved God enough to turn their lives over to Him, and allowed God to use them in special ways. In one way we are all special because God created each of us, and He loves each of us. We will become more special when we allow God to use us. Will you do that?

3. God does not force anyone to do anything. He lets us decide for ourselves whether to do right or do wrong. This is what we call "free will." When your mother or dad tells you to do something, you know that you have a choice. You can either obey your parents so that they will be pleased with you, or you can disobey them so that they will have to punish you. It is much nicer to please them, isn't it? Obedience works the same way with God—He lets us choose, but we will be much happier if we obey Him.

4. God uses us to tell and show other people how much He loves us all. That is a *very* special and very important job! We can share that job no matter how little we are. You can be kind and patient with your friends and tell them that God loves them. How can you show them that you love them too? How can you show your parents that you love them? How can you show God that you love Him?

5. How does it make you feel to know that "God is on your side"? Can you tell God how it makes you feel, and thank Him for loving you?